Puffin Boo[...]

The Lost Me[...]

and

The Wishing-Nut Tree

There were once a fisherman and his wife who lived in a little stone house by the sea. It was all as neat as could be, especially the kitchen, which had a dresser, two chairs, a carved oak settle, and a wooden cradle. The cradle was empty, but that didn't worry the fisherman and his wife, for they were very happy as they were, until they found an enchanting little merbaby lost in the cove. Then they realized a baby was just what they wanted after all . . . if only they could forget the mournful sounds from the waves of someone grieving deep in the sea.

The second story tells how an old man leaves each of his three sons a wishing-nut, and how comically wrong even the best-laid wishes can turn out.

These charming stories were first told a long time ago, when Margaret Baker, who wrote them, and her sister Mary, who partnered them with delightful silhouette drawings, were both young, but each has the true fairy-tale feeling and the satisfying kernel of deeper meaning that will enrich and outlast generations of children.

The Lost Merbaby

AND

The Wishing-Nut Tree

MARGARET BAKER

ILLUSTRATED BY

MARY BAKER

PUFFIN BOOKS

Puffin Books, Penguin Books Ltd, Harmondsworth, Middlesex, England
Penguin Books, 625 Madison Avenue, New York, New York 10022, U.S.A.
Penguin Books Australia Ltd, Ringwood, Victoria, Australia
Penguin Books Canada Ltd, 2801 John Street, Markham, Ontario, Canada L3R 1B4
Penguin Books (N.Z.) Ltd, 182-190 Wairau Road, Auckland 10, New Zealand

This edition first published by Kestrel Books 1979
Published in Puffin Books 1980

The Lost Merbaby first published in 1927
The Wishing-Nut Tree first published in 1942
Copyright © Margaret and Mary Baker, 1927, 1942, 1979

All rights reserved

Made and printed in Great Britain by
Richard Clay (The Chaucer Press) Ltd,
Bungay, Suffolk

The Lost Merbaby

ONCE upon a time there was a fisherman and his wife who lived in a little stone house by the sea. It was not very big, but that was no matter, for it was so neat and pretty that no one could wish it to be different. There was a creeper climbing on the wall and a pot of flowers in each little window; and in the little kitchen there was a dresser with rows of blue platters, and two chairs and a round table and a carved oak settle, and by the fireside was a wooden cradle.

But the cradle was empty.

'A baby would be so troublesome,' said the fisherman's wife. 'How should I keep my little house neat and clean with a baby to mind?'

'A baby may be very well in its way,' said the fisherman, 'but we are happier as we are.'

Every day the fisherman set the sails of his boat and went out to sea; and every day his wife went busily about the little house and when her work was done she took her knitting and sat beside the door. She would see the clouds wandering across the sky, and the waves breaking on the sand, and the sea-gulls wheeling above the cliffs, and then at last she would see the little boat come sailing into the bay, and run down to the beach to wave a welcome to the fisherman so soon as he should be near enough to see it.

'Who could be happier than we?' said they.

Not so far away there was another little home, but it could not be seen from the fisherman's house however hard one looked, for it lay under the sea. It was only a sandy hollow among the rocks, but it was set about so prettily with sea-weeds that it could not be bettered; and in the hollow lived three little mermaids and a mer-baby.

The little mermaids loved the baby dearly, but for all that they often found her a great deal of trouble.

'Oh dear!' they would sigh, 'how glad we shall be when she is grown up! She is sure to want us if we swim far away, and see how she plays with our sea-weeds and spoils them, and how she disturbs the sand in our little hollow when we have taken so much care to make it smooth. She

is the most beautiful merbaby that could be, but she is rather a nuisance sometimes.'

Now it happened one day that they found a round basket, such as the fisherfolk use, floating on the waves.

'Here is a cradle for our baby!' they cried. 'When we want to play we can lay her inside and the waves will rock her to sleep.'

So they took the basket and stopped up the holes and lined it with sea-weed and put the baby inside. The baby laughed and crowed with delight, and the little mermaids swam down to

their home in the hollow among the rocks. They tidied the sea-weed and smoothed the sand on the floor, and then they swam back to the cradle and peeped inside, and the baby was fast asleep.

'See how useful a cradle can be!' they said. 'Now we can play where we like, for she will not need us for a long, long time.'

But the little mermaids had forgotten all about the wind and the tide, and while they were gone the basket was carried far away. It was carried so far that at last it came to the foot of the cliffs near the fisherman's house, and there it rolled over and the merbaby slipped into a rock-pool all among the anemones.

When the fisherman came sailing home he saw something shining at the foot of the cliff, and as soon as he had brought his boat to land he went to find what it could be. It was the merbaby's hair shining like polished gold in the sun.

'Good lack!' cried the fisherman. 'What have we here?'

The merbaby was very tired of being all alone and it held out its little arms and cried to be taken up.

What was there left for the fisherman to do but to lift the baby from the pool and hurry home with it as fast as he could?

The fisherman's wife was just as surprised as he. She took the baby in her arms and hushed it and sang to it and coaxed the smiles back into its face.

'How it laughs and crows!' she cried. 'Look, its eyes are the colour of the sea, and what a dear little tail it has! It is nearly as beautiful as a real baby.'

Then they pulled out the wooden cradle and put the baby in it, and there it lay crooning happily to itself. The fisherman's wife kept running to look at it and sing to it, and the baby laughed to see her and tangled its tiny hands in her hair; and the fisherman made it a rattle and brought it shells for toys.

That was all well enough, but away under the sea things were not going well at all. The little mermaids had come back from their play and were looking everywhere for the merbaby.

'Have you seen her?' they asked the plaice who were lying half-buried in the sand.

The largest plaice flicked the sand off himself, for it is not polite to speak to anyone with

only your eyes showing. 'I have not seen any merbabies for quite a long time,' he said, 'but that may be because I only see things that are above me, on account of my eyes. Perhaps you have noticed my eyes are both on one side of my head,' he said proudly, 'we are not like other fishes.'

'Our baby was in a cradle,' explained the little mermaids. 'It was only a round basket, but it rocked up and down on the waves and sent her to sleep as well as a real cradle could have done.'

'Something that might have been your cradle floated overhead a little while ago,' said the plaice. 'That is the way it went. Now if my eyes had been one on each side of my head I should never have seen it.'

Away swam the little mermaids, but no sign of the merbaby could they find.

Presently they met a porpoise. 'Have you seen our baby?' they asked, and told him all the tale.

'This is a very sad business,' said the porpoise. 'Come with me and we will see what can be done.'

So they swam away together and asked all the fishes they met for news of the merbaby. Not one of them had seen her, but they were so sorry for the little mermaids that they all joined in the search.

The fisherman stood at the door of his house. 'There is no wind,' said he, 'but how strangely the sea is tossing!'

How could he know the waves were made by the mermaids and the fishes as they looked for the lost merbaby?

'Let us go to the rock-pools under the cliffs,' said the little mermaids.

The lobsters came out of their holes to see what was wanted.

'We have lost our baby,' said the mermaids. 'We used to think she was only a nuisance, but now she is lost we are sure we can never be happy till she is found.'

The lobsters waved their legs in surprise. 'We never take any notice of our own babies,' they said, 'so of course we do not mind losing them; but we are sorry for you all the same, since you are so sorry for yourselves.'

'There is a nasty wicker thing over there that

might be your baby's cradle,' said the eldest lobster. 'It looks too much like a lobster-trap for my taste, but as you are not lobsters perhaps you will not mind going near it.'

The little mermaids swam to where he pointed with his claw and there among the rocks they found the basket they had used for a cradle. But there was no merbaby in it.

A big crab came sidling towards them. 'You look as miserable as if you had just cast your shells,' he said. 'What can be the matter?'

Then the mermaids told their sorrowful tale all over again and the crab was very sad for them. He went up and down the rock-pools explaining what had happened to everything he met, to the fishes and shrimps and sea-horses and even the whelks, but not one of them could tell him anything.

At last he came to the anemones. 'Have you seen the merbaby?' he asked.

'How could we see it?' asked the anemones. 'We haven't any eyes.'

'How dreadful to have no eyes!' exclaimed the crab, popping his own in and out with horror at the thought.

'It is not dreadful at all,' said the anemones. 'We have dozens of feelers and they are much more sensible than eyes, we think.'

'But I can't help being sorry for you,' said the crab. 'Why, even if the mermaids' baby was here you could not see her, and she is well worth seeing, they say; her hair is golden yellow and her eyes are the colour of the sea.'

'What does it matter what colour hair may be as long as it is hair?' said the biggest anemone crossly. 'There is a piece twisted round one of my feelers now and it is most uncomfortable.'

The crab brought the mermaids to look. He twiddled his eyes in great excitement. 'See what I have found!' he cried.

One of the mermaids gently untangled the hair from the anemone's feeler, and the hair was so fine and so shining that it could have belonged to no one but a merbaby.

'Our baby has been here,' they told each other, 'but where can she be now?'

The puffins came waddling along to see what was the matter. They looked very wise indeed when the mermaids had finished their tale.

'Now we come to think of it,' began one.

24

'We don't often think, you know,' said the others, 'but when we set our minds to it we think to some purpose.'

'When we come to think of it,' said the first puffin again, 'we saw the fisherman pick a mer-baby from that very pool where you were talk-ing to the anemones.'

'Oh, tell us what he did with her!' cried the little mermaids.

'He took her home, of course,' said the puffins. 'Your baby is not lost any more because we have told you where she is.'

And they waddled away.

'Alas!' cried the mermaids. 'We are scarcely better off than when we did not know where to find her. The fisherman's house lies far beyond the reach of the waves, and we can only go where the waves carry us.'

Then the mermaids lifted themselves out of the water. 'Sea-gulls! Sea-gulls!' they cried.

'Fly to the fisherman's house and tell us what has become of our baby.'

So the sea-gulls flew away across the sand and round and round the fisherman's house.

'Surely there is a storm coming,' said the fisherman, 'else why should the gulls fly so near us and cry so loudly?'

How could he know they had come to see what was done with the merbaby?

'The fisherman has put the baby in the cradle and his wife is tending it as though it was her own,' said the sea-gulls when they came back.

Then the little mermaids began to weep and sigh. 'If they grow to love her they will never give her back to us,' they sobbed.

The merbaby heard them and began to wail pitifully.

'Hush, hush!' soothed the fisherman's wife. 'It is only the moaning of the sea before bad weather, but I could almost weep myself for the sorrowful sound of it.' And she shut the window.

How could she know the merbaby cried because the little mermaids were weeping for her?

As was but to be expected, the news of the merbaby soon spread among the fisherfolk and they one and all made some excuse to come tapping at the fisherman's door.

The fisherman's wife showed the baby proudly. 'Look what beautiful eyes she has!' she would say. 'And see her tiny hands and the shining of her hair!'

'Yes, yes,' said the fisherfolk, 'but it is a great pity she has a tail.'

'It is a very beautiful tail,' said the fisherman's wife. 'And there are so many people with feet that to have a tail is to be rather distinguished.'

'A tail will be very awkward when she grows up,' said the fisherfolk shaking their heads. 'Why don't you put her back in the sea?'

'How cruel that would be!' cried the fisherman's wife. 'She is far too tiny to care for herself. Besides, we love her too much to part with her now.'

So the merbaby lay from day to day in the wooden cradle and cooed and crooned to itself. The fisherman would leave the mending of his nets to play with it, and his wife sang it gay little songs as she went about her work and ran to kiss its tiny hands and cover it with caresses.

'How could we think a baby was too much trouble!' they wondered. 'A baby is the loveliest thing in the world.'

The little mermaids had no heart now to tend the sea-weeds that grew in their home among the rocks, nor to smooth the sand on the floor and make all neat and tidy; they had no heart to talk to the fishes, nor to play as they had done before.

'But perhaps the fisherman's wife may tire of her,' they thought.

So every day they swam to the foot of the cliffs. 'Sea-gulls! Sea-gulls!' they cried. 'Fly away and bring news of our baby!'

And every day the sea-gulls told how the fisherman's wife was fondling the baby as though it was her own.

'Alas! Alas!' wept the little mermaids. 'We shall never see our baby again.'

And every day when the merbaby heard the sound of their crying she began to wail and would not be comforted.

Then the fisherman would shake his head and ponder, ''Tis strange,' said he, 'the moaning of the sea is like the sound of someone weeping.'

His wife, too, would ponder on the strange-
ness as she tried to hush the baby's crying, and
she pondered so long that in the end she could
not help but find the truth.

'Hark!' cried she. 'The baby weeps in answer
to the sound. It is no moaning of the waves she
hears, but the sorrowing of those who have lost
her,' she said, and she lifted the baby from the
cradle and kissed her on this cheek and that, and
ran with her to the shore. There sat the little
mermaids weeping, and when they saw the
fisherman's wife they held out their arms.

'Give us our baby,' cried they. 'We cannot play, nor sing, nor be happy till we have her again.'

'Sorrow no more, here is your baby,' said the fisherman's wife, and she kissed her over and over and gave her to them.

But when she came back to the little house and saw the empty cradle, she fell to weeping as sadly as ever the little mermaids had done.

'It is my turn to sorrow now,' she said.

And the fisherman could find no words to comfort her for he was as sad as she.

But the little mermaids were happier than they had ever been before, and they swam up and down with the baby to tell all the sea-creatures of their good fortune and to thank them for their help.

'You look much happier than you did,' said the crabs, 'but it is rather hard to understand why you should be so glad to have such a troublesome thing as a baby.'

'That is because you do not understand family life,' said the puffins. 'We think a great deal of our babies, but of course they are much nicer than merbabies because they have down and feathers.'

'And wings,' added the sea-gulls. 'We cannot imagine what use arms can be.'

The anemones began to close as soon as the mermaids came near. 'We are glad you have found the baby, since it pleases you so much,' they said hastily, 'but do take her away or we shall get all over hair again.'

The fishes looked at the merbaby curiously. 'Her tail is very fine,' they admitted, 'but a fin or two would improve her.'

'Or having both her eyes on one side of her face,' said the plaice.

'But of course if you are satisfied with her there is nothing more to be said,' added the porpoise, and waved his flipper as he swam away.

The little mermaids hugged and kissed their baby. 'Fancy thinking she is not perfect!' they cried. 'Only the fisherman and his wife know how to love her as we do, and now they are

sorrowful because we have taken her back again.'

So sometimes they would swim to the little bay and call, and the fisherman's wife would hear them and come running to the edge of the sea. Then the mermaids would give her the baby, and she sat on the rocks to play with it and fondle it.

'It is so lonely with an empty cradle,' she would sigh.

The little mermaids would sigh for sympathy. 'We will come again soon,' they promised.

But one day when they swam to the bay, though they called and called, the fisherman's wife did not come running out to greet them.

'What can have befallen her?' they asked one another.

Then they lifted themselves out of the water. 'Sea-gulls! Sea-gulls!' they cried. 'Fly away across the sand and tell us why the fisherman's wife does not hear us calling.'

So the sea-gulls flew round and round the little house as they had done before.

'You need not sorrow longer for the loneliness of the fisherman's wife,' they said. 'There is another baby in the cradle; it has feet instead of a tail and its eyes are the colour of the sky, but she does not seem to mind, nor does the fisherman. They have not heard you call because they are too happy to hear anything but their own joy.'

Then the little mermaids swam back to the hollow among the rocks.

'Now we can all be happy all the day long,' they said, 'for there is no one left lonely and sorrowing. And some day we will go again to the bay and the fisherman's wife will show us her baby and we will love it next to our own.'

The Wishing-Nut Tree

THERE was once a miller who had three sons, Rick and Nick and Hickerydick, and which of the three was the laziest it would be hard to tell. They never did a day's work that they could help, and if there had been any way of making a living without the trouble of earning it, the mill might have dropped to pieces for all they cared.

Now the miller was a very old man and with every month that passed he grew older. One night he called his three sons together.

'Look on the top shelf of the cupboard when I am dead and gone and you'll find an old teapot,' he said; 'look in the teapot and you'll find a bag; look in the bag and you'll find three hazel nuts, one for each of you. If you are clever enough to use them aright you are all set up for life.'

Rick and Nick began to laugh at the idea of three hazel-nuts being of use to anyone, and so, for that matter, did Hickerydick.

'Make fun of me if you choose,' said the old miller, 'but have a care what you do. The nuts are wishing-nuts, and if you crack them and wish aloud you'll get whatever you asked to have in less time than it takes to snap your fingers. 'Tis a long story how they came my way and my breath is all too short to tell it, but they've been in that teapot for fifty years and there they are still.'

'What!' cried Rick and Nick, 'do you mean us to believe that you've kept three wishing-nuts for nearly a life-time and done nothing with them?'

The idea was so amusing that they laughed louder than ever, and so, for that matter, did Hickerydick.

'No doubt you are very clever,' said the miller, 'but for myself I could never decide on three wishes that suited me. If I wish this, then thought I, next week I'll be fretting because I haven't wished for something else and so I left well alone and got what I needed with my own two hands. But if you can find a wish apiece that you'll never regret, there are the nuts in the

teapot and you may laugh at me for a simpleton all the rest of your lives.'

By-and-by the old miller died. Rick and Nick went about with sorrowful faces, and so, for that matter, did Hickerydick, and the house and the mill seemed sadly empty and forlorn; but in the midst of their grief they were always thinking of the wishing-nuts and trying to decide what they wanted most.

Rick was the first to make up his mind and he took down the old teapot, opened the bag and picked out the largest nut.

'I'm going to make myself rich,' said he; 'if I have plenty of money I can buy everything else I may need.'

'But stop a minute! Stop a minute!' cried Nick and Hickerydick. 'If you wish for a fortune it is sure to prove too small, for the more one has the more one wants.'

'I've thought of that,' said Rick with a wink; 'and I've thought of a great deal more.' He put the nut on the floor and crushed it with his heel. 'I wish that every time I put my hands in my pockets I may find twice as much money in them as there was before.'

Nick was almost ready to crack his own nut and wish the same thing, and so, for that matter, was Hickerydick, but by good fortune they decided to wait a little and see how things went.

Rick put the wish to the test at once and plunged his hands deep into his pockets; he pulled two pennies out of one and three out of the other. He put his hands into his pockets again and pulled out ten pennies, and then twenty, and then forty, and twice as many, and twice as many, and twice as many again!

'You silly fellow!' shouted Nick, beginning to rock with laughter. 'You should have put a golden guinea into your pocket before you wished; now you'll have to work all day to get enough money to buy anything worth while.'

Rick went red with anger, and then he turned pale with fear. Every time he tried to empty his pockets they grew twice as heavy and before he had sense to stop he was dragged to the floor by the weight of them and held there as helpless as if the mill-stones were on top of him.

Nick and Hickerydick laughed till the tears ran down their faces, and as there was no magic about their hands they emptied Rick's pockets for him and stood him on his feet.

'Whatever shall I do?' he cried. 'If I put my hands in my pockets again I'll be crushed to death with pennies and what sort of an end is that for a man?'

'You'll have to have your pockets sewn up,' said Nick and Hickerydick and for fear of any accident they got needles and thread at once.

So that was the end of the first wishing-nut and little good there had come of it, for Rick was left without pockets for the rest of his life and all the fortune he had gained was a pile of pennies that would not fill a corn-sack and a coat dragged out of shape till it was hardly fit wear for a scarecrow.

Nick was the next to take the old teapot from the cupboard-shelf and pick out a nut.

'Are you sure you know what you want?' asked Hickerydick.

'I'm going to be able to have everything I want for always,' said Nick with a knowing waggle of his head. He cracked the nut with his hands. 'I wish that every wish I wish aloud may come true!' he cried.

'Why didn't I think of that myself?' growled Rick enviously, and Hickerydick's first thought was to crack his own nut and say the same thing. 'But perhaps it will be better to wait a while and see what happens,' he said to himself.

Nick wished for a purse full of money and a velvet cloak and a pair of top-boots and a horse to ride, and they were there before he could draw breath again.

At first he could only gasp 'Oh!' and 'Ah!', but when he had had time to recover a little from his surprise he led the horse out of the mill kitchen and rode up and down with Rick and Hickerydick at his heels. He admired himself and his new possessions to his heart's content and if he thought of anything else he fancied, such as a fine house, or a diamond ring for his finger, or a statue of himself in front of the mill, he had only to take the trouble to wish for it aloud.

Then matters began to grow a little awkward.

'I wish all our friends and neighbours were here to see what a fine figure I cut,' he said thoughtlessly, and immediately he was surrounded by a crowd of people, staring and pointing and exclaiming at sight of such grandeur.

For a minute he was rather put out, but unexpected visitors, even though they be counted in dozens, need cause no anxiety to people who can have whatever they want. He wished for a dining-hall large enough to hold

them all and for a dinner of turkey and plum-
pudding, and then invited everyone to sit down
and make themselves at home.

At first all went well, but presently Nick
had a mind to make everyone think that a fine
dinner was nothing to a man of fortune and how
better could he do that than by finding
fault?

'Tut-tut!' he said loudly; 'the turkey has been
cooked five minutes too long and I wish the
bread-sauce had more pepper in it.'

The wish was granted as quickly as the others

For a minute he was rather put out, but unexpected visitors, even though they be counted in dozens, need cause no anxiety to people who can have whatever they

had been and in less than half a minute all the company were coughing and choking and trying to ease their throats with gulps of water.

As soon as he could speak Nick wished the plates and the turkey thrown on to the rubbish heap and a fresh dinner of salmon and green peas served in their place. The guests were just beginning to eat with relish and to treat the pepper mistake as an excellent joke when Nick spoilt it all again.

want. He wished for a dining-hall large enough to hold them all and for a dinner of turkey and plum-pudding, and then invited everyone to sit down and make themselves at home.

'I never knew such awkward things to carry to one's mouth as peas,' he grumbled; 'I wish they'd stick to the forks!' – and they did!

They stuck so firmly that they would not come off again and not one could be eaten.

Nick roared for the plum-pudding and in it came, but as ill-luck would have it he burnt his mouth with the very first spoonful. 'I wish the pudding wasn't so hot!' he cried, and every helping became as cold as a stone!

Some of the guests began to complain of their treatment, and some began to make fun. Rick had to hold his sides, and so, for that matter, had Hickerydick, and Nick grew purple with anger and shame. 'I wish every one of you was home again and that all I've wished for was at the bottom of the sea!' he shouted; 'and I wish I may never say "I wish" again!'

The friends and neighbours were whisked away faster than they had come, and the horse, the fine house, the velvet cloak, the diamond ring and all the rest disappeared in a twinkling and a great splash they must have made as they dropped into the waves.

So that was the end of the second wishing-nut and all Nick had to show for it was a tongue that could not say 'I wish' no matter how he tried.

Hickerydick did not mean to waste his chances as his brothers had done and he did little but think the whole day long and left Rick and Nick to do all the work of the mill.

At last he found a wish that seemed as if it could not go wrong and he took the last nut from the teapot and cracked it between his teeth.

'I wish,' said he, 'that when I plant the kernel it may grow overnight into a hazel-tree covered with wishing-nuts that when I crack them will each give me a wish.'

'Why didn't we think of that ourselves?' growled Rick and Nick.

'Because you're not as clever as I am!' said Hickerydick, and out he strutted to plant the kernel in front of the mill-house.

Next morning he leapt out of bed with the first cock-crow and put his head out of the window. The biggest hazel-tree he had ever seen almost blocked the view and from every twig hung a cluster of nuts.

He dressed in such a hurry that he forgot half his clothes and ran out of doors.

'Thousands and thousands of wishes and all of them mine!' he sang, dancing with glee. 'Now I can have whatever I like, whenever I like!'

He picked a nut and cracked it and wished for a penknife with a dozen blades because he wanted to see if the tree was all he meant it to be, and the knife was in his hand in a twinkling.

'They're wishing-nuts all right!' he cried, and gathered them by handfuls as he shouted to Rick and Nick to come and share his good fortune.

After that Hickerydick had only to crack a nut to have every idle wish come true. He wished the mill would work by itself all day; he wished for three new fishing-rods; he wished they were all sitting on the bank of the river without the trouble of walking there; he wished the gnats would go and buzz somewhere else; he wished he might catch the largest fish ever seen thereabouts, and when the sun grew hot, he wished they were home again.

'And the best of it is,' he cried, 'that when all the nuts in my pockets are used I've only to gather a fresh supply and then I can start wishing again as often as I can think of anything we want.'

The brothers had the laziest day that three lazy men could desire, and then at night Hickerydick wished they were in bed and even cracked another nut to wish the candle out to save him the bother of blowing at it.

''Tis a grand life and no mistake,' said he as he sat in the shadow of the mill next morning and listened to the mill-stones grinding busily while the sacks of grain emptied themselves into the hoppers without anyone having to lift them.

'The nuts will last longer if you don't waste them wishing the same thing over and over,' said Rick.

'Why not wish that the mill works by itself like this every day?' asked Nick; 'and that we shall have a good breakfast every morning and find ourselves snugly tucked in bed every night?'

'No, no!' cried Hickerydick; 'I've seen enough of that kind of wish. Suppose we didn't want any breakfast one day, or, what's more likely, that we didn't want to go to bed, and there's the wish making us do things against our will. By the time there are only a few hundred nuts left on the tree I'll know what it's wise to wish for and what it's wise to leave alone and then I'll be able to set up the three of us for the rest of our lives.'

Rick and Nick could not but agree that this was a sensible way to look at things and they settled down to enjoy themselves. They dozed and dreamed for hours together and when they were tired of doing nothing at all Hickerydick wished they were at the Fair, winning a coconut with every throw at the Aunt Sally and seeing all there was to be seen; or that they were sitting on the village green talking with everyone who went by; he even wished for the fiddlers and morris dancers to come and amuse them, and very astonished the dancers were to find themselves capering in front of the mill instead of making hay in the meadows below.

One afternoon as the brothers were dozing their time away at their favourite spot on the river bank, Nick turned over with a yawn and said he wanted a cushion for his head.

'You'll have to manage without one unless you get it for yourself,' said Hickerydick, feeling in his pockets. 'I've used all the nuts I gathered this morning except a little one and I expect I shall want that for something for myself before long.'

'What!' cried Rick in horror. 'Do you mean to say we can't have anything else till you feel inclined to go home and shake down some more nuts?'

'It's very uncomfortable without a cushion now I've begun to want one,' yawned Nick.

'I have it!' cried Hickerydick. 'Why didn't I think of it before?' He cracked the nut. 'I wish my pockets were filled again,' he said, and immediately they were so crammed with wishing-nuts that they could not hold another.

After that he never troubled to go nut-gathering again; he simply wished his pockets full as often as they emptied, which left him more time to waste than ever.

'We shall have to start being careful with the wishes soon,' said Rick one morning as they left the mill.

'How dreadful!' said Nick.

'No need to bother,' said Hickerydick with a grin. 'When we get to the last nut I'll wish it to grow into another wishing-nut tree and we'll go on like that for always.'

'But how can you be sure you don't use the last nut for something else by mistake?' asked Rick anxiously.

'I've attended to that,' said Hickerydick; 'I've wished that the last nut shall not come into my pocket, but shall hang on the tree till it is picked.'

Rick and Nick looked at their brother in admiration; there could be no doubt he was a clever fellow.

So the nut-cracking and wishing went on as before and the three lazy men had scarcely to move a finger, day in, day out; there was no need even to go to the trouble of thinking what to get with the last few nuts, for they were going to have as many more wishing-nut trees as ever they wanted.

At last came the time when Hickerydick wished his pockets full and nothing happened.

'What's the matter?' asked Rick and Nick.

Hickerydick turned his pockets inside out and felt the lining of his coat for fear a nut should have slipped through a hole. 'We must have come to the last one,' said he; 'there's nothing for it but to walk home and pick it and start another tree growing.'

'You might have managed things better than to get us stranded a mile away from the mill-house,' Rick grumbled.

'You're not quite so clever as you thought you were,' sneered Nick, and they sighed and complained all the way back, and so, for that matter, did Hickerydick.

The hazel-tree was a sorry sight; it was stripped and bare as if it were the depth of winter, but on the highest branch there still hung one last wishing-nut.

First they tried to shake it down and then they tried to knock it down with stones, but the nut would not fall.

'I know what's the matter with it!' cried Hickerydick; 'I wished the last nut would hang on the tree till it was picked and so we shan't be able to get it in any other way.'

They took it in turn to climb the tree, but the branches were too slender to bear their weight and the mill ladders were no use because they were too short.

'We'll have to chop the tree down, that's all,' said Hickerydick.

Away they ran to get the axe, but when they found it the handle was broken and the edge was blunt and it took a very long time to put them to

rights. When at last the axe was fit for use the three brothers hurried back to the hazel-tree, anxious not to lose any more time in getting a second crop of wishing-nuts to keep them in luxury and idleness.

As they came round the corner of the mill-house Rick and Nick stopped in horror, and so, for that matter, did Hickerydick.

Swaying on the topmost twig of the hazel was a squirrel, and it picked the nut before they could so much as cry 'Stop thief!', cracked it in its teeth, threw down the shell and ate up the kernel.

'I'll catch him! I'll pay him out!' shouted Hickerydick and began to hack at the tree with the axe.

'Don't do that!' shouted Rick and Nick; 'if you cut it down it can't bear nuts another year!'

But it was too late! The wishing-nut tree came crashing to the ground and the squirrel spread its tail and jumped to the mill-house roof and disappeared.

So that was the end of the miller's nuts, one, two and three, and there was nothing left for the brothers to do but put on their aprons and caps again and go back to work in the mill.

'I wish the nuts were still in the teapot,' sighed Rick, 'and then we could start all over again.'

'We wouldn't make any mistakes with our wishes if we had another chance,' said Nick.

'I'm not so sure of that,' said Hickerydick; 'it seems to me that wishes are teasing things and we should have done well to leave the nuts in the teapot where we found them.'

Rick and Nick shook their heads at that, for they did not mean to admit the old miller had been wiser than all of them. They groaned and grumbled as they went about their work and tried to believe they were very unhappy, but if the truth be told, they were thoroughly tired of doing nothing at all –

And so, for that matter, was Hickerydick.

ABOUT MARGARET
AND MARY BAKER

Margaret and Mary Baker were born in the 1890s and describe their early occupations as being 'daughters-at-home' with their Quaker family. They have lived in various parts of the country during their lifetime, and have taken great delight in travelling in Great Britain and in Europe, but they have now settled in a Cotswold village where they are constantly visited by their many great-nieces and great-nephews.

Their first book together was published in 1923, and this marked the start of a partnership that lasted twenty-seven years and produced thirty-seven books. Published in Great Britain and in America, the books that Margaret wrote and Mary illustrated met with great success.

Ill health forced Mary to give up her fine and intricate silhouette drawings, but she is still able to continue water-colour sketching, to her great joy.

CARROT TOPS
Joan Wyatt

Fifteen stories of everyday events like making a jelly, growing a carrot-top garden, visiting Granny – all tinged with the make-believe that young children love.

MATTHEW'S SECRET SURPRISES
WHERE MATTHEW LIVES
Teresa Verschoyle

Happy stories about a little boy exploring his new home, a cottage tucked away by the sea, with all its secrets and surprises. (*Originals*)

A GIFT FROM WINKLESEA
Helen Cresswell

Dan and Mary buy a beautiful stone like an egg as a present for their mother – and then it hatches into the oddest animal they ever saw!

TELL ME A STORY
TELL ME ANOTHER STORY
TIME FOR A STORY
MORE STORIES TO TELL
ed. Eileen Colwell

Stories, verses, finger plays for young children, collected by one of the greatest living experts on the art of children's storytelling.

THE STORY OF HOLLY AND IVY
Rumer Godden

A magical Christmas story about three special wishes made by a lonely orphan girl, a doll without an owner, and a policeman's wife with no child to share her Christmas tree.

STORIES FOR UNDER-FIVES
STORIES FOR FIVE-YEAR-OLDS
STORIES FOR SIX-YEAR-OLDS
STORIES FOR SEVEN-YEAR-OLDS
STORIES FOR EIGHT-YEAR-OLDS
ed. Sara and Stephen Corrin

Celebrated anthologies of stories specially selected for each age group and tested in the classroom by the editors.

GRIMBLEGRAW AND THE WUTHERING WITCH
Barbara Sleigh

Prince Benedict and Princess Yolanda are captured by the giant Grimblegraw, who has been enchanted by an evil witch. They must find her and trick her into lifting her spell.

ADVENTURES OF SAM PIG
SAM PIG AND SALLY
SAM PIG GOES TO MARKET
SAM PIG GOES TO THE SEASIDE
YOURS EVER, SAM PIG
Alison Uttley

Five sets of comical stories about Alison Uttley's best-loved character, who always tries to be helpful.

DINNER AT ALBERTA'S
Russell Hoban

Arthur the crocodile has extremely bad table manners – until he is invited to dinner at Alberta's.

OLD DOG, NEW TRICKS
Dick Cate

'I'm too old to learn new ways,' said Billy's father when he lost his job at the coal mine, and Billy's new dog seemed to feel the same way, but a new neighbour helps him solve his problems.

THE WORST WITCH
Jill Murphy

Mildred Hubble is the most disastrous dunce of all at Miss Cackle's training school for witches. But even the worst witch scores the occasional triumph!

MRS PEPPERPOT'S YEAR
Alf Prøysen

'Goodness,' said the little girl in hospital when she saw that the nice old lady who was tucking her in had suddenly shrunk to a few inches high, 'you must be Mrs Pepperpot!' 'Right first time,' said Mrs Pepperpot, 'and now it's your turn to help me.'

Who is he?

His name is Smudge, and he's the mascot of the Junior Puffin Club.

What is that?

It's a Club for children between 4 and 8 who are beginning to discover and enjoy books for themselves.

How does it work?

On joining, members are sent a Club badge and Membership Card, a sheet of stickers, and their first copy of the magazine, *The Egg*, which is sent to them four times a year. As well as stories, pictures, puzzles and things to make, there are competitions to enter and, of course, news about new Puffins.

For details of cost and an application form, send a stamped addressed envelope to:

The Junior Puffin Club
Penguin Books Limited
Bath Road
Harmondsworth
Middlesex UB7 ODA